A NOTE TO PARENTS

When your children are ready to "step into reading," giving them the right books is as crucial to their development as giving them the right food to eat. **Step into Reading®** books feature exciting stories and information reinforced with lively, colorful illustrations that make learning to read fun, satisfying, and rewarding. We have even taken *extra* steps to keep your child engaged by offering Step into Reading Sticker books, Step into Reading Math books, and Step into Reading Phonics books, in addition to fabulous fiction and nonfiction.

Learning to read, Step by Step:

- **Super Early** books (Preschool–Kindergarten) support pre-reading skills. Parent and child can engage in "see and say" reading using the strong picture cues and the few simple words on each page.
- **Early** books (Preschool–Kindergarten) let emergent readers tackle one or two short sentences of large type per page.
- **Step 1** books (Preschool–Grade 1) have the same easy-to-read type as Early, but with more words per page.
- **Step 2** books (Grades 1–3) offer longer and slightly more difficult text while introducing contractions and clauses. Children are often drawn to our exciting natural science nonfiction titles at this level.
- **Step 3** books (Grades 2–3) present paragraphs, chapters, and fully developed plot lines in fiction and nonfiction.
- **Step 4** books (Grades 2–4) feature thrilling nonfiction illustrated with exciting photographs for independent as well as reluctant readers.

Remember: The grade levels assigned to the six steps are intended only as guides. Some children move through all six steps rapidly; others climb the steps over a period of a few years. Either way, these books will help children "step into reading" for life!

www.randomhouse.com/kids/disney

Library of Congress Cataloging-in-Publication Data
Gaines, Isabel.
Pooh's Easter egg hunt / written by Isabel Gaines; illustrated by Studio Orlando.
—1st Random House ed.
    p.   cm. — (Step into reading, step 1)
Summary: Winnie the Pooh goes on an Easter egg hunt with a hole in the bottom of his basket.
ISBN 0-7364-1208-5
[1. Easter—Fiction. 2. Easter eggs—Fiction. 3. Teddy bears—Fiction. 4. Toys—Fiction.]
I. Milne, A. A. (Alan Alexander), 1882–1956. II. Studio Orlando. III. Title. IV. Series.
PZ7.G1277 Pof 2002
[E]—dc21
00-068961

Printed in the United States of America January 2002   10 9 8 7 6 5 4 3 2 1

STEP INTO READING, RANDOM HOUSE, and the Random House colophon are registered trademarks
of Random House, Inc.

Winnie the Pooh

Pooh's Easter Egg Hunt

A Step 1 Book

by Isabel Gaines

illustrated by Studio Orlando

Random House 🏠 New York

"Happy Easter!"
Winnie the Pooh
called to his friends.

It was time for
the Easter egg hunt.

Rabbit said,
"Whoever finds
the most eggs wins.
Get ready,
get set . . . go!"

Pooh, Piglet,
Roo, Eeyore,
and Kanga walked
into the woods.

Pooh found a yellow egg
under some daffodils.
He put the egg
in his basket.

But Pooh did not know
his basket had a hole.
The egg fell out
onto the grass.

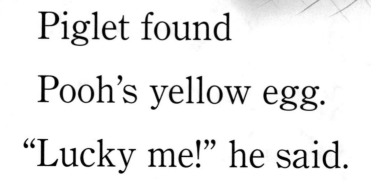

Piglet found
Pooh's yellow egg.
"Lucky me!" he said.

Then Pooh found
a purple egg
behind a rock.
That egg slipped out, too!

Roo found Pooh's egg.
"Oh, goody!" he cried.
"Purple is my
favorite color!"

Pooh found a green egg
and put it in his basket.
But he did not
see it fall out.

Tigger found
Pooh's green egg.
"I am on my way
to winning!" he said.

Pooh found a red egg.
It fell through the hole,
too.

Eeyore found

Pooh's red egg.

"Oh, my," he said.

"I found one."

On the side of a hill,

Pooh found a blue egg.

"How pretty!" he said.

Pooh walked up the hill—
but the blue egg rolled
down the hill!

Kanga found
Pooh's blue egg
next to a log.

"Time is up!"
Rabbit shouted.
Everyone ran over
to see who had won.

Pooh's friends
each showed their
Easter eggs.

Pooh looked inside
his empty basket.
"My eggs seem to be
hiding again," he said.

Piglet looked at the basket.
He poked his hand
through the hole.
"I think I know why,"
said Piglet.

"You can have my
yellow egg," said Piglet.
"It was probably your egg
before it was mine."

"Thank you, Piglet,"
said Pooh.

"And you can have my
purple egg," said Roo.

"Here, Buddy Bear,"
said Tigger.
"Tiggers like to win
fair and square."

Eeyore gave Pooh
his red egg.
"It was too good
to be true," said Eeyore.
Kanga said,
"Take mine, Pooh!"

Rabbit counted the eggs.

"Pooh is the winner!"

he cried.

"You win an Easter feast."

"Is there enough
food for everyone?"
asked Pooh.

"I can make more,"
said Rabbit.

"Is there enough honey?"
asked Pooh.

"Of course!" said Rabbit.

"Hooray!" said Pooh.

The feast was great fun.

Everyone ate Easter eggs!

But Pooh liked

the honey best!